T0196499

.

DOGMAIL

DERRICK TILLIS

authorHOUSE®

AuthorHouse™
1663 Liberty Drive
Bloomington, IN 47403
www.authorhouse.com
Phone: 1 (800) 839-8640

Published by AuthorHouse 04/24/2017

ISBN: 978-1-5246-0169-0 (sc)
ISBN: 978-1-5246-0168-3 (e)

Print information available on the last page.

This book is printed on acid-free paper.

CONTENTS

CHAPTER 1

In all aspects of life, I have never been thrilled enough to speak about the things that have occurred over the last couple of days. But in the end I found that even with it's surprising moments, it was all for the best. I'd love to tell you who or why the story is being told and who I am, but that may just spoil the fun. So I'll leave it unto you to decide in the end who I am and why you love me so much. If that last part didn't make sense that was the whole point. You'll catch on soon. Now we'll begin with a guy named Jake. He still makes me laugh.

Mr. Butler: Jake…

Jake: Yes sir, Mr. Butler sir, I'm right here, on time, at your service, right here sir.

Mr. Butler: I need you to run a whole route today on your first day of work to see how long it will take you, and that will help me decide if I should keep you or let you go. Now do you think your capable of this task Jake?

Jake: Yes sir, Mr. Butler sir, you can count on me.

Mr. Butler: Now Jake there's one other thing I want you to be very aware of.

Jake: Yes sir, I'm all ears.

Mr. Butler: The one thing that you don't want to run into or know about Jake, it's a mailman's worst nightmare. We've lost the best we've had to this evil, disguised as friends of man. When deep down inside they are put here to take us all out, these beings, these monsters, these, these, "Dogs." That's why I've equipped you with the tools to separate these beasts, don't trust them Jake because as soon as your back is turned, we'll you know the rest. Now get out there and show the world why we're the best at what we do, Deliver.

Jake: Yes sir, I sure will, you can count on me.

Jake happily exiting his bosses' office to what he sees as a journey or mission that he is placed in position to dominant. Bag on his shoulders, keys twirling on his finger without a care in the world, as if he wakes up to heaven and the clouds are filled with candy everyday.

Back at him CeCe and Nalii are at it again, doing what they do best.

Nalii: Oh my God, CeCe stay out of my room.

CeCe: The remote was in your room.

Nalii: No it wasn't.

CeCe: Yes it was.

There is a brief pause before the storm and a loud explosion is heard coming from the kitchen.

Nalii: CECE.

CeCe: My pizza is in the oven.

Nalii: That's it, I'm calling daddy.

CeCe: So!!!

Nalii: I'm going to tell him what you said too.

CeCe: So!!!

Meanwhile, Jake is happily trotting along not realizing he's dropping mail, making mistakes, but very chipper about landing the job he always wanted. To be a mailman is Jake's greatest accomplishment of his life, funny but true. Jake's phone rings.

Jake: Hello, Hello, Hellooo.

Nalii: Dad, CeCe is destroying everything in my room and blew up the kitchen!!

Jake: Hum, Hum, Uhh, okay sweetheart, I'll take care of everything when I get home.

CeCe: No he won't.

Nalii: See daddy? She's doing it again.

CeCe: See daddy she's doing it again. Listen, if you stop now and hang up the phone I'll help you clean up you choirs as well as my own, but if you insist on fighting me, your going to make it difficult for me to watch my shows and I'm going to make it difficult for you to call another number again, if you get my drift. Now tell daddy we played nice or I won't be nice.

Nalii: Okay daddy, false alarm, you know how I am sometimes and how moody we both are, we are growing girls. Daddy what time you coming home?

Jake: Well I guess if you girls are okay than.

Jake pauses for a second.

Jake: I may be able to work the overtime that everyone is being so nice about letting us have, okay goodbye.

Nalii: No daddy, wait, wait, daddy. daddy.

Jake hangs up the phone, well it's overtime that is much needed, some folks are just nice for no reason at all, he says to himself. Jake is close to 9 hours into his shift when the phone rings…

Mr. Butler: Jake!!! I need you to take Glen Road and Summerhill. Think you can do that??

Jake: Sure sir, I'm on it, you can count on me I'm going to…

Before Jake could finish his sentence, Mr. Butler hung up the phone. He got his answer so anything else really didn't matter. So Jake is off, smile across his face and again, dropping mail, but that ole Jake didn't prepare for the surprise he was about to get, who could? Jake is an honest man, yet gullible at times, okay most of the time, you know what, all the time. But for the first time in his life, Jake was actually wiry about something, cautious thinking, almost worried; this feeling was something new to him, and for good reason. The house that he is about to enter gave him the creeps… But why? Jake opens the gate, the front door is nearly 20 yards away, as Jake thought about his journey to and through the yard, that 20 yards turned into a mile. Jake starts to sweat, slowly onward toward the front door, almost tip toeing. He takes a deep swallow due to his nervousness and puts his head up with confidence that he does not have at the moment, Superman with no cape, Popeye with no spinach, Marching, as he looks around the yard, against these fenceless walls, set up like military walls, he sees signs that say, "Beware of Dogs." Jake cringes and tries to ignore his fear, but it is too late. He runs for the door hoping someone would be home to greet him before the beasts that were awaiting his arrival did. The bloodhounds of all no-good deeds. Once inside the corridor, he slouches down slowly wiping the sweat from his face. The front door opens slowly but only to his relief, he'd be hoping that someone was there to save him from his own mind or these hounds that taunt his mind.

Sir: "Hey their Mr. Mailman, would you like some water or lemonade? Sorry you'd walk all this far to bring me my mail."

Jake: Well how else would I be able to get it to you? It's my job to make sure it's where it belongs.

Sir: Well I'd say you nice, thank you very much.

Jake: No problem!!

Sir: Being that the mailbox is right behind the gate, I mean if you look right next to the lock. In the future all you got to do is reach your hand in. But it's greatly appreciated again, have a great day, thanks, Bye now!!

The door slams like the dungeon doors in the early hundreds after a prisoner sought to meet his doom. Jake frantic, he panics, sounds coming from the bushes, bad breathe seeping and causing a cloud of fog almost blinding Jake. He can't see his hands in front of him, his feet lost in the thick soot. Jake turns around and heads for the front gate with all that he can muster, out from the bushes come two ferocious beasts behind, Jake screams in horror.

Jake: NOOOO!!!

The beasts are inches from catching the prize and maybe a meal, when Jake leaps over the wall, his mailbag snagging the fence boomeranging him back against the metal doors, and behind him, through the fence come the two most highly anticipated threats to all human kind. Ones tag reads "Sky," the other "Pumpkin." Two of the cutest smallest, happiest dogs you'd ever meet. Jake relieved and happy that his imagination was only that.

Jake: Whew!! That old boss of mine is such a kidder. Why would I get all puzzled?

Shortly after Jake is finished at work, while driving home, he comes across a pack of dogs, 12 to be exact, all different types, some with dog tags, some without. One in particular stops right in front of the car and looks directly in his eyes and growls, Jake turns his head toward the passenger side and whistles as if he sees nothing and no one. When the pack of dogs are no longer in his view he wipes his forehead and starts his drive once again to go home.

Upon entering the door, both his daughters greet him. Nalii hugs him and helps him out of his uniform and makes his plate ready and brings him some fresh pajamas for bed. On the other, CeCe hugs his around his waist and as usual doesn't let go and within 5 minutes you'd hear snoring and she has to be peeled off of his legs. Jake has to be dragged to be as usual after a hot meal and Nalii, well seems to be in a place of comfort. Her dad and sister remind her of he dolls she had as a toddler, easy to put to sleep, the only thing that's different with the clothes are they come in a larger size. While asleep, Nalii sees that as a great time to talk.

Nalii: Daddy?

Jake: Hmm, yes sweetheart.

Nalii: I have a school trip to see some schools I may want to attend at next years scholar events pick rally, all I need is the money to go and I'll be gone for 3 days.

Jake: Okay sweetheart, whatever you want. Make sure you take your sister so she's not upset, and push her on the swings; she likes the swings, and the pool.

Not knowingly agreeing, Jake will wake up remembering the conversation and will make himself an honest man.

CHAPTER 2

The following day, Jake wakes up as he does every morning, prepares the girls breakfast and gets them ready for the day with grandma Lizbeth.

Grandma: Okay girls, we are going to spend the day making cookies and cupcakes and gardening. Oh… This is going to be so much fun!!

CeCe: Grrr, do we have to? (CeCe utters quietly) I want to watch TV.

Nalii: Oh, CeCe really? That seems to be the only thing you want to do everyday.

CeCe: Grandma, do you have an icepack?

Grandma: What do you need an icepack for sweetheart?

CeCe: I don't, Nalii will need one for her headache shortly.

Nalii: You're a very angry person.

Jake leaves home on his way to work, today is a special day. Jake has no mail but he has deliveries. Jake can move at his own pace, not so much to do on Saturdays, he's happy.

Mr. Butler: Now Jake today should be very nice, smooth sailing, you should be able to deliver all of these packages with no problem.

Although Jake had planned to get out of work early, things did not actually turn out that way.

Jake: Whew!! One more delivery and that is it.

Jake approaches his last stop. Ignoring the beware of dog sign, he rings the bell several times, but there was no response. He hears voices in the backyard, Jake doesn't like to interrupt, but this is a non-fragile package. Jake slowly makes his way to the back of the house. A picket brown wooden fence is standing between Jake and his final stop. As Jake climbs over the fence, he falls into the bushes. There are voices and then they stop. One of the voices asks, "Did you hear that?"

Roy: Jack go and see what that noise was?

Jack: I'm on it, Roy.

As Jack sniffles around the ground, his nose is leading him to the bush where Jake is. As Jack gets closer, Jake slowly opens the bushes with two hands. What he sees is not normal, eyes widening, and his hair is standing on top of his head. Jack barks at the bushes.

Roy: Hey Jack, you find anything?

Jack: I don't see anything, but my nose has never lied to me.

The moment Jack turned his back, Jake jumped out from behind the bushes to make a run for it. Jake leaps over Jack and runs towards the gate that seems open on the opposite side of the yard. He's been spotted by a pack of dogs.

Roy: Look boys, we have company, let's welcome our new friend.

The pack takes off behind Jake. Jake jumps over the fence, in front of the house and into the street. He then turns around to see if the dogs are coming. Only one dog approaches, with not a soul in sight. The dog speaks to Jake, in a very low and threatening voice.

Roy: Hey there friend. Seems you walked into the wrong backyard, but don't worry you don't have to hold your new found secret.

Jake: You. Can. Talk.

Roy: O Yeah!! But you won't be around to see that too much. I have a nice bone-yard with your name on it.

Jake: Listen, I can explain. Actually I don't have anyone to explain anything too. Listen, I have daughters who like dogs. I'm just a mailman. I mean no harm.

While Jake is trying to reason with Roy, Jack gets an earful when Jake says he has daughters who like dogs. Jack is astray dog, the pack isn't. Jack jumps in front of Roy, giving Jake enough time to escape.

Roy: Come here ya little pup, what do you think your doing? You know what kind of trouble we could be in if they knew we could talk?

Jack: I don't think so street mutt. I have a bone to pick with him and maybe it's going be sooner than later.

Roy looks down on the ground and sees Jakes driver's license with his address and home number. He calls Nose!!

Roy: Nose! Sniff this and tell me where we going this weekend.

Nose: Do you think I can finish eating first boss? I love spaghetti.

Jack: I think it's pointless to go bother someone like him, I mean look at him, and he's obviously no threat. I mean you can put a leash on him and walk him.

Roy: Jack, if you think he's worth our fate than you put your paws up for him and remember to sweep. I'm not letting this go. You're either with us or your not, make a decision now!!

Jack: I'm with you Roy.

Roy looks at Jack, unsure that Jack will make the right decision being that he's not an owned dog without tags. Roy's thinking he may need to watch Jack from here on out.

Jake reaches home after work. Never before worried or frightened due to his gullible, and naive ways. He walks in silently, not saying a word to his girls, which brings

CeCe to ask a question, which is something she never does. Something all so new, concern.

CeCe: Dad are you okay?

Jake: Fine honey! I just had a rough...

Before Jake finishes his sentence, he and Nalii turn and look at CeCe, confused but still in aww!!

CeCe: What are you two looking at!

Both Jake and Nalii respond with, "Oh nothing, nothing." CeCe makes her way back to the couch and back to her T.V. shows. Nalii and Jake both peek from the kitchen, still in shock.

CeCe: Okay, I'm assuming your going to sit there and watch me for about ten minutes, so while you're at it, make me a grilled cheese please. Bring me some juice, chips, and an icy, thank you.

Jake: Well honey that's too much junk food.

CeCe doesn't respond, she just gives Jake a look. The look that tells him she's serious and taking no prisoners.

Jake: Okay honey, whatever you want.

Nalii: Mom would not be happy about this dad.

Jake: I know, she's probably yelling at me right now.

Jake making his way to his bedroom where he closes the door very slowly, missing his wife, he picks up an old photo of her and sits on his bed, hugs the picture and takes to his pillow, lamp goes out. Jake is off to sleep. His daughter Nalii stands in the doorway and watches her dad as he sleeps. She walks over to him and puts the picture; he has cradled in his arms, on the nightstand and covers him with a blanket.

Nalii: Sweet Dreams Dad.

Grandma: You know your dad really loves you girls. He just doesn't know how to keep you both smiling. He tries his best, he will always try his best, but one day you'll both move out, go to school and this house will be empty. Just memories and he won't have anything to come home to but he's happy right now, that you girls are still his little princesses. Be gentle with him. Now come on and let me tuck you girls in, and we'll eat waffles in the morning.

Both Nalii and CeCe wish grandma a goodnight and lay down with smiles on their faces. Grandma makes her way to the living room and opens up the photo album of Jake and the family. She smiles, yet she looks sad. She feels sorry for her son. She looks at the pictures until she fall asleep.

CHAPTER 3

The following morning, Jake wakes up and walks into the kitchen where the girls and grandma are eating breakfast.

Grandma: Have a good sleep son?

Jake: Yes ma'am, I feel great, so I think I'll stay with you and the girls today. Lets go to the air.

The girls are excited, CeCe doesn't show any emotion but she's very happy on the inside. Jake even decides to call Mr. Butler and tell him he won't be in to work today.

Mr. Butler: Hello? Hello?

Jake: Mr. Butler, sir I won't be in today. I'll come in tomorrow and thank you.

Mr. Butler: Jake you need to…..

Before Mr. Butler can finish his sentence, Jake hangs the phone up on him.

Jake: Okay ladies, pack your go bags and water balloons cause we're going to have some fun.

Nalii: Last on to the car is a rotten egg.

CeCe: Really Nalii?

Jake and the girls along with grandma all scramble to be the first ones to the car.

When Jake and his family reach the fair they are greeted by security and a patrol dog named Nose. Jake spots Nose and Nose quickly whisks the hair from in front of his eyes to get a better look at him. As Jake and Nose pass each other, they both give each other a very odd stare, slowly pulling the car into the parking, both yet to take their eyes off of each other.

Nalii: Dad? Why do you keep looking back at that dog?

Jake: Oh, nothing sweetheart, I didn't know the fair would have an animal outside the cages here that's all.

Nose: Humph!!!

As Jake and the girls approach the first ride, Jake notices the stray dog Jack scavenging for food. CeCe also spots him and yells.

CeCe: Daddy, Daddy, Daddy look!! That dog doesn't have a home, he's going through garbage, can we keep him?

Grandma is seen feeding Jake hotdogs and popcorn. When the ride is done, Jake and the girls approach grandma with her newfound friend.

CeCe: Can we keep him Dad?

Jake replies with No, animals are sometimes dangerous. He gives Jack a look, he's not sure he can trust Jack. Jack also looks back at him with sadness and as the family walks away, Jack whispers to Jake.

Jack: Sorry!!

Jake is unsure of his decision at this point but doe not go back on his decision. Meanwhile with Nose on a break, he finds time to make a call to Roy.

Nose: Hey Roy! You would not believe who's at the fair right now; I mean you would not believe in a million years.

Roy: Who?

Nose: I mean you wouldn't believe me if I told you.

Roy: Nose!! Shut up and tell me who.

Nose: Oh yeah, yeah!! The mailman, the mailman.

Roy: Is that right, Hmmm…

Nose: Yeah, that's right, that's right.

Roy: Good job Nose. I'll see you later tonight; we're going to get the boys together.

Nose: Yeah! Yeah! Gotta go, my best friend is back.

Nose hangs up the phone leaving Roy to ponder is next plot. Jack on the other hand, he bumps into Nose.

Nose: Hey Jack, what's going on? I just spoke to Roy about the mailman.

Jack: Honestly Nose I don't care, I have my own problems.

Nose: Hey, what's your problem?

Jack: You really wanna know? I'm tired of being a stray. I'm tired of being the black sheep of the bone-collectors. While you all have somewhere to go I find myself looking for empty boxes when it rains or a house with a barn when it snows and scavenging for scraps, while you guys enjoy the good life. Just leave me alone.

Jack runs out of the park, Nose looks on. It's almost time for the park to close and Jake is getting the girls ready to go home.

Nalii: Dad?

Jake: Yes honey.

Nalii: Why can't we have a dog?

Jake: I told you already, dogs can be dangerous.

Nalii: That dog didn't seem so dangerous, just hungry. If mom were here she'd let us have a dog, besides we don't have company to play with when you're at work.

Jake: Well you have your sister sweetheart.

Nalii: You know what I mean.

The ride home is nothing more than silence, the kids left the house happy only to return home saddened. When getting out of the car Jake asks Nalii to help with the stuffed animals they won playing games, but she ignores him and goes inside.

Jake: CeCe honey, you wanna help with the stuffed animals, it'll look nice in your room.

CeCe: I don't want those stuffed animals, they don't play, they just sit still.

Jake sighs while dropping his head, feeling as if he is disappointed at the girls.

Jake: I try, but I can't say yes to everything.

Grandma: You don't have to say yes to everything but think about this, when children are full they don't need to be fed. Go inside and get some rest dear, you did good today. They still love you, don't worry yourself.

Jake walks inside and sits next to CeCe on the couch, he doesn't say anything, she doesn't say anything either. She moves over next to her dad and wraps his arm around her and he smiles. She has her moments but Jake knows that the girls love him. But to actually get a hug from CeCe says a lot. Her hugs are like therapy.

The next day, Jake is off to work. Like every morning, forgetting about the dogs and last nights upsets, he sets his eyes on completing his job at a reasonable time so he can go shopping for a pet for the children. When he gets to work he's greeted by his boss and a route that he may learn late that he does not want.

Mr. Butler: Jake!! Come in my office, and close the door. I have a job for you.

Jake: Yes sir, anything you need. What do you need?

Mr. Butler: You'll be working with Monroe on Clover Lane today. Any problems call the office, you got that?

Jake: Sure sir, I'm on it.

Monroe: Hey Jake, your with me today, grab your pepper spray and dog net, we're gonna be busy.

Jake thinks to himself, why the dog net? Not knowing that Roy had made a call acting like he was his owner and requesting Jake to make the deliveries in his neighborhood.

Jake: Why do we need a dog net Monroe?

Monroe: Cause where we're going, they'll be more dogs than an ant farm and they love to chase us guys.

Jake: Okay, in that case, I'll grab the extra pepper spray in Mr. Butler's office. I hear they're afraid of him.

Jake and Monroe head to Clover Lane to make the deliveries as requested by their boss. Once reaching the first house in the neighborhood, Jake notices Nose in the very next yard along with Chester. He doesn't panic; he pulls out the pepper spray, almost as if he wanted to warn the dogs without having to speak to them.

Jake: Now you boys be good, I just want to drop off your owners mail with no problems and be back on my way. I don't want any trouble. Nose and Chester aren't budging; they both just give Jake a cold hard stare.

Monroe: They seem to like you very much or your carrying doggie treats.

Jake: I kind of wish I was, but they seem like great dogs to have.

Nose: Wow, he seems like a very nice guy.

Chester: You don't get all sentimental on me, we have a job to do, remember?

Nose: Oh yeah!! Kind of got stuck in the moment. Can you scratch my back?

Chester: Listen if you don't straighten up I'm gonna take off your flea collar and tell Roy to let you go deep sea diving in the boneyard.

Nose: No need, not necessary.

As the mailmen get closer to Roy he gives all the dogs the signal. Every dog within a two-block radius is on standby. Jack approaches Jake and gives him a serious look. Jake can't seem to grasp what Jack is saying. So finally, Jack yell out.

Jack: RUN!!!

Jake drops the mail and takes off running leaving Monroe back trying to figure out who let out the yell.

Roy: After them boys, and string up Jack. I knew he wasn't one of us. The stray is going to the pound or the boneyard.

Jack: This way. They're not going to stop running after us. We have to lose them.

Jake: When is this going to stop? It'll be bad for my job if I keep this up.

Jack: Just be quiet and run. We're almost there.

Jake: Almost where?

Jack: My old home.

Jake: And why are we going there?

Jack: I have an idea, and my old friend may be able to help you.

Roy, Nose, Chester and he rest of the bone collectors are right behind Jake and Jack when suddenly Jack slips through a small crack in a picket fence that stands 10 feet off the ground. Jake is a bit big and cannot fit.

Jake: Help, I can't squeeze through.

Jack: Go around. I'll open the fence. Hurry!!

Roy: There he is, get him before he gets in the fort.

Chester: I'm on him. I got him Roy.

Just when Chester was about to sink his teeth in Jakes backpack, he's clobbered with a broomstick. An older gentleman with a patch on his eye and one hook for a hand comes out.

Roy: He made it. Don't worry fellas we'll get him. We'll get you too Jack. You trader. You hear that? All the dogs in the neighborhood are gonna know you're a sellout.

Jack sits still looking down at the ground, disappointed in him self but the anger outweighs the disappointment.

Otis: Well those dogs have a way with how they handle business, ha! How did you get caught up in the grit and grime, if you don't mind me asking?

Jake: I walked into a card game; I guess I disturbed the peace.

Otis: Hey Jack!! How you been little buddy?

Jack: Do you really wanna know Otis?

Jake: I thought I was imagining all of this but I wasn't. They really do talk.

Otis: Yep, every last one of em!! They all just keep it amongst themselves. Seems you have a lot of enemies now Jake. You wouldn't believe where it got me.

Otis: I was young at the time.

Otis going into a memoir of the past and how his accident occurred.

Otis: When I stumbled across a pack of dogs that I'd pass by everyday behind gates and fenced in walls. I didn't know much better than so I'd tease them and throw things at them, until one night on my way home I came across a huge dog by the name of Roylex. He was the leader of the pack of dogs throughout the neighborhood and his rival was one half-breed named Karnasge. They fought for the respect and both were very territorial but in the end Karnasge was taken down by the locals. He was a wolf you see. He had a pup with a local dog named Sugar that Roylex thought belonged to him. I took care of Karnasge after my accident. I wouldn't be here today if he hadn't saved me but he did, and he left behind a pup. I wanted to keep him but he was too wild, wanted to be free. Never knew his dad but I et you some fried frog legs if you saw the eyes on that dog and you looked at Jacks eyes, you'd know. I didn't have to be told, but Karnasge told me to take care of his pup. And I'm an honorable man. My losses could be worse if it weren't for him.

Jake: So you're saying that Jack is a wolf?

Otis: Yep! Half-breed. That's why he doesn't have a home, nobody would take a wolf, too risky, but when I did, his dad stayed but he refused to when came time.

Jake: So why did you run with those pack of animals?

Jack: Cause I belonged with them. Who wants a wolf around their children? I had no choice.

Jake: You always have a choice. You could have stayed with Otis.

Jack: I wanted a family, and children. I watched how all the other dogs were loved and how they protected the children and how the children protected them. Why can't I have that?

Jack puts his head down with a look of guilt and shame, remembering when his daughter asked him if she could have Jake.

Otis: Well buddy, your always welcome here, you know that.

Jack: I know, but I want more, I'm sorry old friend.

Otis: Aww, don't worry about it. You deserve the best, your father would have been proud.

Jack: I'd like to believe that Otis.

Jack walks out into the backyard of the apartment complex and looks off into the moon. Saddened, ashamed and lost.

Suddenly, Jake's phone rings.

Jake: Hello, Hello?

Roy: Hey there Jake buddy, old pal. How's it hanging?

Jake: Why are you calling me from my daughters phone?

Roy: Oh, I don't know, maybe because your mom loves dogs and we love your family.

Jake: If you lay a paw on them.

Roy: You'll do what? All you have to do is get home before Cinderella loses a shoe and we can discuss what to do with you and that trader half-breed Jack. Sounds good?

Jake: I'll be there. I'll be there soon.

Otis: You might need some help and I'd advise you to take the little wolf out there if you want to make it out in one peace.

Jake: What can one dog do?

Otis: When threatened he's no ordinary dog. He's his fathers' son. Just trust me on this one. Wolves protect the pack; they don't know any other way once they've become family.

Jake: But he's not family.

Otis: Let that decision be up to you. Maybe he can squeeze in somewhere, maybe you need him to. Just think about it.

Jack comes back into the apartment and senses something terrible.

Jack: What's wrong?

Jake: Oh, nothing. I need to be getting home now; you have a good night and good luck. Thanks Otis and thank you Jack.

Jake makes out the door in haste.

Jack: Otis what happened?

Otis: Pup, that mailman is in trouble. Roy has his family as we speak and he's with the pack.

Jack: No!! I gotta go Otis. If I'm not back by morning, I just want you to know I appreciate all that you've done.

Otis: Anytime kiddo. Now go get that family. Your dad would be proud again I say. I know I am. Give me one for the road.

Jack opens the door to the moon behind him and for the first time he lets out a howl that shakes the town.

CHAPTER 4

Back at Jakes house!!

Grandma: CeCe can you help me bring the treats out for these pups?

CeCe: Aww man, I don't like these dogs. I want the one from the carnival.

Nalii: CeCe just help grandma out, you're always so difficult.

CeCe: You really want to make me angry Nalii?

While the girls are inside bickering, the pack is outside awaiting Jake and Jack. When suddenly Jake enters the backyard.

Roy: The mailman is home. Look fellas he's a good boy, he listens without having to be trained, HaHaHa!! But where's the mutt?

Jake: He's not with me.

Roy: What do you suggest we do about that sir?

While waiting for an answer Jack leaps on top of the wall.

Jack: I suggest you leave here, all of you. Before there's trouble.

Roy: And who's gonna cause us trouble? You're a small guy with a big heart but that's not enough.

Jack: Maybe for the pack, but for you I may be a bitt too much.

Roy: Is that right?

Jack: That is!!

Jake tries to run in the backdoor and before he can reach the stairs the pack is standing in front of him, snarling and bearing teeth. He yells out.

Jake: Girls? Mom?

They all come to the backdoor to see what's going on.

Jake: Stay back. I just wanted to see you.

Grandma: What's going on out here?

Nose forgetting like he does, utters loudly.

Nose: Nothing grandma, we're about to see a fight.

Grandma faints, Nalii screams and CeCe smiles and says…

CeCe: See dad, I knew it wasn't a regular dog. He talks too right.

Jack: You better believe it. And I'm gonna take care of you until I can't owl at the moon anymore.

Roy: Than let's get this show on the road, shall we?

Roy charges Jake causing him to tumble off the wall, while the pack sits back for an opportunity to jump in. Jake snaps at Roy not biting or even touching him.

Roy: Let's face it, your no match for me. Your not even a pure wolf, your only a half-breed, and I'm gonna bury you in the boneyard.

Jack: I'd like to see you try it.

They both lock on to each other fearing the worst. Jake pulls out a stun gun from the shed.

Jake: Let him go.

Otis: Jake stay back. These dogs have had this coming for some time now.

Jake: Where'd you come from?

Otis: Oh, I wasn't going to let you walk these dogs all by yourself friend.

Jack and Roy still struggle and fight. Roy is unsure as to how Jack is getting stronger. His hair standing on end, fangs irregular to ordinary dogs and he just keeps getting stronger.

Roy: You can't beat me mutt. I'm the leader of the pack.

Jack: But I protect a pack. Your no champion, you're a coward, and a bully just like your father.

Roy: You mutt. How dare you talk about my old man?

Roy jumps toward Jack, Jack moves and rips Roy's collar off after slamming him on a rock.

Roy: You can't beat me coward. I own these dogs, I own you.

Jack: You've never owned me. I just didn't know the importance of real family. Now I do, and this pack is over. Any Objections?

All the dogs, utter No softly as they look at each other and Roy in disbelief.

Jack: Now get your friend and leave this place, and never come back. You have no business in or around this neighborhood. This is my territory and my family's.

CeCe comes storming out of the house and grabs Jack around the neck.

CeCe: See daddy, I told you he was good. Can I have him?

At this point Jake dares him self to say no.

Jake: Yes, yes you can sweetheart. He couldn't leave if he wanted to.

Otis: Guess you've found what your looking for buddy. I'm happy for ya! Would you mind if I bring your dads picture to you? So everyone can see who you are and why.

Jack: I'd rather you bring a copy but only if your in it with him.

Otis: Oh yeah! Sure, I have a bunch of those. He was my best friend. I even got some with Sugar too, oh yeah! Yes sir.

Nalii: Now who does that remind you of?

Grandma, CeCe and Nalii answer.

Grandma, CeCe, Nalii: DAD!!

Grandma: Well if dogs talk, I wonder if cats can.

Jake: No they can't but they're very smart listeners and loyal friends as well.

Jack: Jack listen, I'm sorry if I...

Before Jack can finish his sentence, Jake hugs him and says.

Jake: Get inside and find yourself a room to sleep in.

CeCe: He's going to sleep in my room.

Nalii: No, in mine.

Grandma: I'm the adult; he's going to sleep in my room.

And the family all argued all night about whom Jack would sleep with. CeCe won of course.

Printed in the United States
By Bookmasters